# Vienna and Venture:
## Tales from the Equine Side

# *Vienna and Venture:*
## Tales from the Equine Side

Written and Sketches by

ANTHONY J. LIGUORI JR.

Order this book online at www.trafford.com
or email orders@trafford.com

Most Trafford titles are also available at major online book retailers.

Printed in the United States of America.

ISBN: 978-1-4269-5036-0 (sc)
ISBN: 978-1-4269-5037-7 (hc)
ISBN: 978-1-4269-5038-4 (e)

Library of Congress Control Number: 2010917779

*Trafford rev. 01/05/2011*

 www.trafford.com

North America & international
toll-free: 1 888 232 4444 (USA & Canada)
phone: 250 383 6864 ♦ fax: 812 355 4082

# TABLE OF CONTENTS

"To my father, Anthony J. Liguori Sr. and my mother,
Madonna (Russo) Liguori.
Thanks for my brain, personality, and sense of humor."

And

"To Annette Vidot, for all her hardwork and
for helping make the Anethonie Horse farm a reality."

# Vienna and Venture:
## Tales from the Equine side

### Volume I
## Starting Out Together

# Chapter 1

## OUR NEW OWNERS

It was a beautiful day at our new home. Venture and I were becoming very used to our surroundings and our human friends. Oh, pardon me, my name is Vienna. We live on a ranch called the Anethonie Stables. The owners are Annette and Anthony. It's a great place to live and raise a family. Life here is as good as it gets. Don't let me kid you though. It wasn't always this way for myself and Venture. You see, when we were first born, Anthony and Annette would come visit us and the other new foals at Ayden's horse farm. In the weeks that followed, it was apparent that they were going to buy us from Ayden. They would come by everyday to handle us and feed us grass. Venture was a little hesitant about being haltered, but they got it on as well as mine too. Somehow we knew we were destined to spend our lives together, and with them.

# Chapter 2

## THE TRAILER

The day came when Ayden was to take us to our new home. We wondered why our mothers had spent the night in a stall with us. Ayden backed the stock trailer to the barn door. There was Annette and Anthony right behind him in their pickup truck. Ayden and Anthony came and took me and my mother Dolly and led us to the trailer. I had never seen one before and was quite nervous. I watched Ayden lead my mom into the trailer, and Anthony and I were right behind them. I paused for a few moments, but eventually stepped up and into the trailer. Ayden closed the dividing door and hopped out. Now it was Ventures turn. Ayden took Dallas, (Venture's mom) and Anthony took Venture. I knew it wasn't going to be easy. Dallas stepped right into the trailer, but when Anthony tried it with Venture, he stopped right at the door and refused to go any further.

Both Ayden and Anthony had to lift his front left leg onto the trailer and push him from behind. Venture suddenly reared up, fell over backwards, and almost landed on Anthony. They tried it once more, and this time he stepped in right next to his mom. Ayden closed the door and Anthony hopped in the truck with Annette. They led us to our new home, which was but a short distance away.

# Chapter 3

## BYE MOM

We pulled into Anthony and Annette's home. It was so pretty, with a new barn, lush green grass, and a nice log home. Venture could hardly control himself, and let out such a loud whinney that it must have been heard by everyone in the county. At four months old, he sounded like a true stallion. The only other noise you could hear was from their dog Butch. He was a big German Sheppard who was just as excited. Some of the local farmers and neighbors were there to catch a glimpse of us. Venture and Dallas backed out first. Ayden and Anthony led them to his new stall. Annette closed the bottom door as Anthony and Ayden stepped out. Now it was my turn. My mother Dolly is no push over when it comes to humans. Anyway, Ayden handled her since she's used to him, and Anthony took me. We all went inside my stall, and again Annette shut the bottom door as the guys went out. Now I know why Venture had been so quiet. There was fresh water in our buckets and nice crisp green hay in our racks. Mmmm. We were so engulfed with eating that we didn't even see them sneak out our moms. By now, Annette had shut the top doors to our stalls. When Ayden started to pull away with the trailer, Dallas started crying for Venture. That's when it hit us. Venture went berserk. Kicking out and rearing up on the walls and yelling at the top of his lungs so everybody heard him. In any event, we both finally settled down, and were thankful that we still had each other.

# Chapter 4

## LOOKING GOOD

In the months that followed, it appeared that our new human friends really loved us. They took such good care of us. Venture and I both saw our first birthday in the spring. By now, Venture was really starting to look like a full grown stallion, my stallion. You see, it was planned that we would start our own family and try to continue Venture's impressive blood lines. Both his Father and Grandfather were champions in their day. Anthony was sure he would follow in their footsteps. In the days that followed, Anthony and Venture would work very hard in the round pen getting him ready for his first show. I worked with Annette in the back paddock. So many humans came to watch. Too many, if you asked me. It always made Venture nervous. After a hard days work, it was comforting to know we would sleep in adjourning stalls.

# Chapter 5

## THE ESCAPE

Then, the most terrible thing happened. This one human they called Mr. Crutch, (who I didn't think Anthony cared for) came to look at Venture. Being impressed at his true abilities, he made an offer to buy Venture. "Nothing doing" said Anthony while chuckling. "This is our stallion for life. We're hoping he'll be even greater then his ancestors." Mr. Crutch was not happy, and started to raise his voice. Anthony did not appreciate this one bit as it was making Venture nervous. He asked Mr. Crutch to leave. "I usually get what I want, and I usually do not take no for an answer." That's the last thing we heard from Mr. Crutch as he sped away.

If butch had not been penned up, I think he would of attacked him. I was feeling a little uneasy that night by this ordeal. Venture didn't seem to care as he was munching on his hay. It was raining pretty hard around midnight, when I saw some truck lights park along the fence of our property. It was pulling a small horse trailer. I didn't think nothing of it, until a man got out and started to cut our fence. I realized it was that mean Mr. Crutch. "Venture! Venture! Wake up. Mr. Crutch is coming. He's coming for you." Butch had not heard a thing as he was in his house, where he always goes when it rains. Mr. Crutch came closer and said, "I always get what I want. Now your coming with me." Venture was standing tall in his stall, when Mr. Crutch opened his door. Before he could hook him up to a lead, Venture bolted through the door and knocked Mr. Crutch to the ground. Venture started to run, when I called to him as loud as I could, "VENTURE". He turned around, came back and opened my latch. We both started running towards the woods, as we heard Mr. Crutch screaming, covered in blood, "Mad horse, mad horse. He tried to kill me. Shoot the beast." We ran straight through the path that leads over the hill, not knowing what to expect. The last thing we saw were the lights going on in the log home, and the last thing we heard was Butch barking like the dickens at Mr. Crutch. I wondered if we were ever going to see Annette and Anthony again.

# *Vienna and Venture:*
# Tales from the Equine side

## Volume II
# A Rough Night

# Chapter 1

## Runaways

It was one thing to be escaping the awful grip of Mr. Crutch, but it's another thing to be called a mad horse and on the run. That's what Mr. Crutch called me as I burst out of my stall door. Hello, my name is Venture, and Vienna my mate was with me as we fled for freedom. It was not the freedom that most living things want, but that of the innocent when being accused of something they did not do. When we saw the lights come on in the cabin, we knew Anthony and Annette would be very upset at what happened. Since I felt Vienna was my responsibility, I told her to just keep running and don't look back. We did just that. The only problem was it was dark and we didn't know where we were going. After what felt like forever, we came to a small clearing where we could rest for a while. We were exhausted.

# Chapter 2

## A Valiant Rescue

After sleeping a bit, we started to graze. Then we heard a crying fawn. Vienna and I ran to the edge of a stream. It was running high and fast due to the heavy rain. We noticed a doe trying to coax her fawn to jump across. She must have been a few days old. The doe was on our side. You could see the fear in the fawns eyes. "Venture, we have to help the babe get across," Vienna said. "You have to do something." All at once, I started to remember how I was afraid of water when Anthony just wanted to bathe me. Now, I was going to rescue a fawn in a raging torrent of water. Right before I was going to enter the water, the fawn made a quick leap to our side, but came up just short of the bank. The swift current took control and the babe was fighting to keep her head above water. I quickly jumped in and was able to run in the stream.

Vienna was running along side the bank, as was the doe. I was just about to put my muzzle under her to nudge her, when Vienna cried out, "Venture, watch out. A fallen tree!" In all of a blink of an eye, I looked up, saw the tree, and hurtled it as I saw the fawn go under. When I landed, I was down stream from the little babe. I got my footing and lifted her right onto the bank where her mom and Vienna were waiting. She quickly fondled her mom as they watched me exit the water. Vienna came right up to me to see if I was alright. "I'm fine" I said. "How's the fawn." The doe and the fawn came up to me and thanked me ever so much. I looked down at the fawn, just as she looked up to lick me on my muzzle. "Why Venture, I think you're blushing." Vienna said. "I am not. That's just a little mud from the stream." The doe thanked us again and they were on their way.

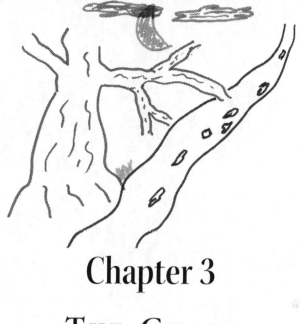

# Chapter 3

## THE CHASE

We started off in the direction of the rising sun as it warmed us. Shortly, we came to a road that led us to the back of a neighboring farm. "Venture, maybe we could get help down there and something to eat." Vienna hoped. "Hold on Vienna. Look by the house. That's the Sheriff." I wasn't sure at the time, and I didn't want to scare Vienna, but somehow I got the feeling he was there because of what happened last night. "Come on Venture, let's" "Wait Vienna, this could be trouble." All at once, the Sheriff and the farmer went to the kennel and let loose two houndogs. As if they knew we were there, they started in our direction. "Quick Vienna. Run. Those dogs have our scent and they're headed right for us." We started off just as we did last night. The forest was very dense and I told Vienna to watch out for the low branches. The howl of the dogs never faded and I knew the Sheriff was right behind them. I told her, "We have to lose them in these woods." With that said, Vienna hit a branch and stumbled to the ground. She was up as fast as she fell. We continued on till it seemed the dogs were far away. "Let's take a breather and listen to what we might hear."

# Chapter 4

## CARING CANINES

When I looked at Vienna, she had a cut on her neck from hitting the branch. It didn't look so bad, but it was bleeding. "Looks like your hurt Vienna. Your bleeding on the right side of your neck." Suddenly, we both heard a twig break, and we became very quiet. Up in front of us were the two houndogs, very much exhausted. They looked at us, and we at them. One of them asked why we were wanted by the Sheriff, and I proceeded to explain the whole incident. Immediately they sided with us and promised they would not tell the Sheriff they caught up with us. Just then one of the dogs noticed Viennas cut and offered to clean it and start the healing process. At first I think Vienna was a little nervous, but eventually she laid down and let the dog lick her wound. The blood stopped flowing and the dog explained that if it started again, to lie on the wound until it stops. Right before they left, I asked them if they ever came in contact with Butch, the dog at the Anethonie Stables, to let him know they met us and that we're okay. Also to explain what happened and try to get Annette and Anthony to come find us and bring us home. Then we heard a whistle and knew the Sheriff was getting close. We said our goodbyes and were on our way. We ran to the west, in hopes the dogs would go the other way. When I looked back, I could see the Sheriff following the hounds in the other direction. I looked at Vienna and said, "It's okay for now, they're going to the east. How's the cut?" She gave me her usual smile and said, "I'm fine. Let's go find something to eat, I'm hungry." We walked a little bit to a clearing and ate the grass right along the woods edge. It was good to relax and soak up the morning sun.

# Vienna and Venture:
## Tales from the Equine side

## Working Horses

# Chapter 1

## A New Task

We stayed by that clearing most of the morning. There was plenty to eat and nobody was chasing us. Hi, it's me, Vienna. My wound had stopped bleeding and didn't look so bad. It didn't bother me a bit. As we were walking along, Venture looked at me and said, "Vienna, take a look at where we are." I was amazed that all around us were nothing but hills and valleys. Since we were never on our own before, we had no idea where we were. It's not the nicest feeling to not know where your home is. We both hoped that Anthony and Annette were on their way to rescue us. Until then, we would have to fend for ourselves and stay out of trouble. As we were just about to enter another stand of trees, we heard a faint whinney. Almost out of desperation. We picked up the pace, and came to a field where a man was beating an old horse with a stick and a whip. Just then Venture gasped in horror, "Vienna, look. It's Mr. Crutch." He was trying to get the old fellow to plow the field, but it was too much for him. We couldn't believe where we were, and what we were witnessing. Finally, old man Crutch gave up and went to have lunch. He left the old horse in the hot sun, hooked up to the plow. He had neither food nor water. As soon as it was safe, we went up to the old guy. "Vienna, help me with this harness." Venture said in a hurry. The poor old horse couldn't even speak. Then Venture wanted me to hook him up to the plow. "Venture. What do you think your gonna do? If Crutch sees you, your done for. And besides, you know nothing about plowing a field." Venture looked at me with a cocky smile and said, "Whats to know. All I've got to do is pull this thing back and forth."

# Chapter 2

## OLD GUS

So Venture started to plow the field, and I took the old guy over to the shade. You should've seen Venture go. Up one side and down the other. All this time, the tired old fellow just slept as if he hadn't slept in years. About two hours later, Venture was done. I went to help him off with the harness, and then we both went to talk to the old horse. He said his name was Gus and hes been plowing this field for twenty two years. "Twenty two years." Venture blurted out. "How old are you?" "I'm twenty seven," said Gus. Venture and I just looked at each other and shook our heads. In the distance we heard someone coming down the road. Gus thought it was his master, so we hooked him backed up to the harness again. He couldn't of been more thankful to Venture as we said goodbye and goodluck. Gus knew we couldn't let Mr. Crutch see us because we explained our situation to him. As we hid amongst the trees, Mr. Crutch started to scream at Gus, but then just stood there in disbelief at the plowed field. We watched as he unhooked Gus and proceeded to actually be nice to him." Good job old boy, lets call it a day." Once they were out of sight, I looked at Venture and said, "You look beat. Lets move on a bit and then you can rest." Venture knew I wanted to get as far away from Mr. Crutch as we could.

We looked at each other and started to trot through the woods. Again we came to a nice meadow where we could graze and rest. Venture walked to a little stream near by, and it seemed he drank every drop in it.

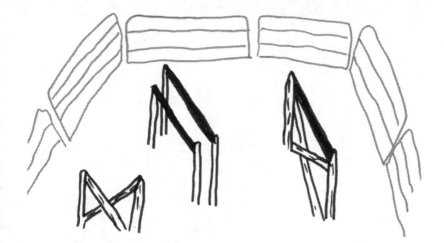

# Chapter 3

## THE SHOW

Vienna and I had been roaming around the country side for a while now. We were starting to get used to the free and easy life. We both terribly missed our owners Annette and Anthony though. Hey, Venture here. Although we did like being on our own, we did want to go home. Vienna always preferred to sleep in a stall. This particular day, we heard a lot of commotion down in the valley. We headed right for it and couldn't believe our eyes. There were a lot of trailers with horses near a big arena, that had a lot of humans sitting around it. From where we were, we could tell this must be a horse show. "Venture," Vienna said with excitement, "This is what you were training for." We watched as horse after horse took their turns in the arena. It was fascinating to see the skill of every horse and their human rider. "Lets get a closer look," I told

Vienna. We walked right down by the trailers just to observe. It was then that we heard a little girl crying out loud. "Mom, Sassys come up lame. How am I going to win the scholarship to the Equine school now?" Vienna and I were not to sure what she was talking about, but it seemed very important to her. We then figured out that her horse had a swollen leg and she could not compete. Vienna didn't realize it at the time, but she looked like Sassys twin. The only difference was the little white sock on Vienna's leg. Everything, even her face was identical. "I think you can help this girl Vienna." She looked at me and glared, "How am I supposed to do that?" "Its easy" I said. "Your gonna take Sassy's place in the arena." "Venture, I'm not sure I can do it." "Trust me." I reassured her. "I used to watch you work with Annette in the back paddock. You can do this." With that said, we walked right up to girl and her mom, and nudged her on the shoulder. "My, my," the mother said. "If she isn't the spitting image of Sassy."

# Chapter 4

## THE BLUE RIBBON

The girl said with anticipation, "mom, do you think I can ride this horse in the show?" "I'm not sure that would be fair, and besides, she has a little white sock on her right side. Someone might notice." I shocked them by scooping up some mud and covered Viennas sock with it. They were twins now. The girl and her mom looked at each other and then at us. "Lets try mom, please." The mom quickly saddled Vienna, who looked like a little girl herself. "I'm not sure I can do this Venture." "You'll be fine," I said. "Just remember what Anthony always taught me. The girl will lead you through the coarse, and you just make a clean jump." Sounds real simple." she said. I nuzzled her and off they went. I stayed out of sight with Sassy. We could see everything where we were, and Vienna strolled through the coarse like a true champion. And a champion she was, as she and the girl were the only team to clear the coarse. They took the blue ribbon and the judge congratulated the girl for winning the scholarship. I forgot myself and let out a whinney that practically shut everyone up. Everyone except two voices in the crowd. "I know that whinney. Its Venture." That was Mr. Crutch who happened to be in the stands. "That's the mad horse who knocked me down." I was already to run but remembered Vienna. The girl realized this and brought her back right away. The girls mom helped Vienna get out of the bridle and saddle. They thanked us and we were off in a flash. When Mr. Crutch made his way to the trailer, he only saw the girl and her mother with Sassy and her blue ribbon. He was fuming because he lost me again. Oh, the other voice that I recognized, was Anthony's. "Venture,

Venture. That's my horse." It was too late to look for him as I knew Mr. Crutch was after us. As we headed up the hill and out of sight, I just had to turn to Vienna and tell her she was something else. "That was some job you did today." "Job. That was no job. That was fun. What excitement." I don't think she understood how close we got to being caught by Mr. Crutch.

## To be Continued...

Printed in the United States
By Bookmasters